Magic Trixie

written and illustrated by
Jill Thompson

Lettered by
Jason Arthur

HarperTrophy® An Imprint of HarperCollins Publishers

This is the last time I am going to call you!

WAKE UP!

I am up...

YOW!

mee-ow!
meow! myow!

RAOW!

WOW!

Five more minutes!

I'm hungry, Trixie!

5

You'll **never** make it down there in time!

MAGIC TRIXIE!

WAIT FOR ME!

Hey, Stitch!

Come on, if you're coming! You can **ride** on the back!

I'll be right...

...down.

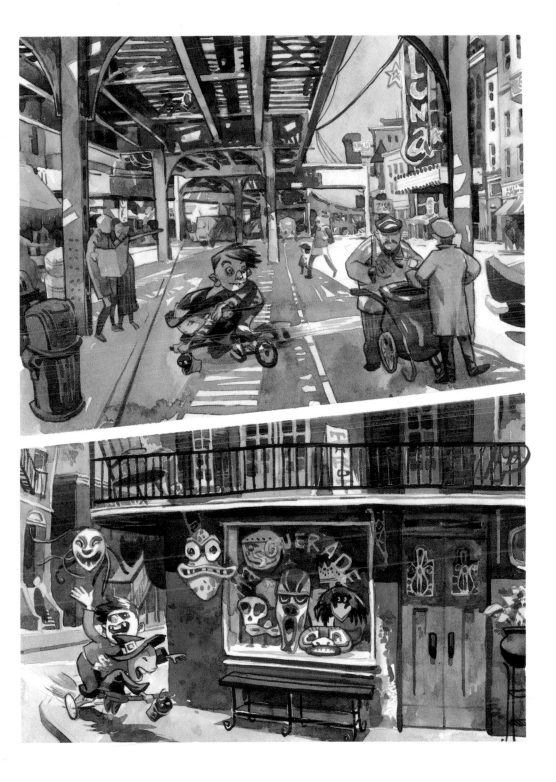

Hi, *Loupie Garou!* Hi, *Nefi!*

Hi, *Stitch Patch!* Hi, *Magic Trixie!*

Nice *training wheels,* Magic Trixie.

It's *landing gear,* LOOP-ie.

How many *times* do I have to tell you?

Oh, yeah... *right...*

RING A DING

RING A DING RING A DING RING

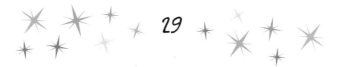

UNROLL

SKRITTCH
SKRITCHa
SKRITCHH

TOSS

FLUTTER

34

42

I also have a **Grampy** and a **Gramberry**, and an **Uncle Monkey** and **Noodle Lou**.

Then there's **Dead Papa**. He lives at the cemetery.

I got a **Tito** and a **Mima**, an **Abuelita**, and The **Old Gentleman**.

What do you call your Gramma or Grampa, **Nefi?**

Your Royal Highness.

44

WATCH THIS, YOU GUYS!

45

HiC HEE HUP

MAGIC TRIXIE!

NO!

PAUSE!

YOU KNOW YOU ARE TOO LITTLE TO USE A BIG WAND!

They all have different **codes** and **passwords**!

Each one is **in tune** with its **owner**!

AW, I don't feel like playing...

INCOMING!

I said forget it, Scratches.

NO! INCOMING! LOOK OUT, TRIXIE!

Tansy!

Oh, that's **different**.

I'm just **rocking** her to sleep.

You said I was **too little** to ride your broom, but Abby Cadabra is **ON the broom** right now and she is **JUST A BABY!**

NOT FAIR!

I'm *doomed*, Scratches, and *NOBODY* cares! They only cared when there was *no baby!*

I care, Trixie. And your *family does*, too.

IF they cared, they'd let me use some *BIG magic* stuff so I could be *special* and not *boring* for show-and-tell!

WOW!

That is a good show-and-tell.

Not as good as mine.

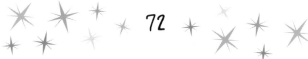

A BABY! It is A BABY!

I can **explain!**

...don't know where you got the idea you could just **take** your **sister** out of the...

...don't even **want** to know what you had that **wand** out for...

...nearly gave me a **heart attack**...

...taught you to be more **responsible**...

Sorry I tattled.

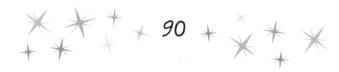

MOTHER!

Can I *use* the *magic wand?*

Magic Trixie! You know you are *too little* to...

It's *not* for *me!*

It's for *ABBY CADABRA.*

She likes to *chew on it* while we *look at* the pictures in the big spellbook!

Read more about
Magic Trixie's adventures in

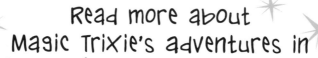

Magic Trixie
Sleeps Over!

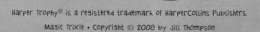

Harper Trophy® is a registered trademark of HarperCollins Publishers.

Magic Trixie • Copyright © 2008 by Jill Thompson

www.harpercollinschildrens.com

Library of Congress Cataloging-in-Publication Data • Thompson, Jill, 1966-

Magic Trixie / written and illustrated by Jill Thompson. -- 1st Harper Trophy ed. • p. cm.

ISBN 978-0-06-117045-4 (pbk. bdg.) • I. Title. • PN6727.T33M34 2008 • 2007024298 • 741.5'973--dc22

Lettering font created by Jason Arthur from hand lettering by Jill Thompson • ❖ • First Edition